Alba
THE HUNDRED
YEAR OLD FISH
LARA HAWTHORNE

**For family and friends on Claremont Road
and the Hamilton House Coexist community.**

B P P

BIG PICTURE PRESS

First published in the UK in 2019 by Big Picture Press,
an imprint of Kings Road Publishing, part of Bonnier Books UK,
The Plaza, 535 King's Road, London, SW10 0SZ
https://www.templarco.co.uk/big-picture-press
www.bonnierbooks.co.uk

ISBN 978-1-78741-292-7

This book was typeset in PiS Creatinin Pro
The illustrations were created with watercolour
and gouache and amended digitally

Designed by Olivia Cook and Nathalie Eyraud
Edited by Joanna McInerney and Katie Haworth

Printed in Malaysia

Alba
THE HUNDRED
YEAR OLD FISH
LARA HAWTHORNE

This is a tale about a one-hundred-year-old fish named Alba.
She lives on the coral reef, and has seen the ocean change
in many ways over her lifetime. Alba's story is inspired by a
real fish called the rougheye rockfish, who was caught off the
coast of Alaska and lived to the grand old age of 205.

There was once a small and quiet town
that overlooked a brilliant blue ocean.

And beneath the surface of
the warm, shallow water . . .

. . . there was a city of coral.
Shimmering fish darted and dived and curious
creatures scuttled into hidden places.

Amid the hubbub swam a young orange fish called Alba, who lived inside an old, spotted shell.

Alba collected beautiful objects.
"I have an eye for such things,"
she would say. Every year on her
birthday, she found something special.

She loved things that were
spotty, stripy and round . . .

. . . bumpy,
spiky and bright . . .

... or curvy,
swirly and small.

Over the years she
grew and grew ...

. . . and so did her wonderful collection.

But as time went by, Alba found fewer beautiful objects . . .

. . . and more strange, unfriendly things appeared.

Alba watched the coral
city change . . .

. . . and every year more of her
friends left.

One year on Alba's birthday, she
realised she had no one to celebrate
with. And even though she searched
and searched, she couldn't find a single
beautiful thing for her collection.

Feeling sad but still determined, she pushed on through the murky water until she was the furthest she had ever been from home.

Suddenly, she noticed something bright,
glowing in the darkness. Swimming closer,
Alba realised it was a pearl. "How wonderful!"
she exclaimed.

It was just out of reach, resting in the most unusual shell Alba had ever seen.

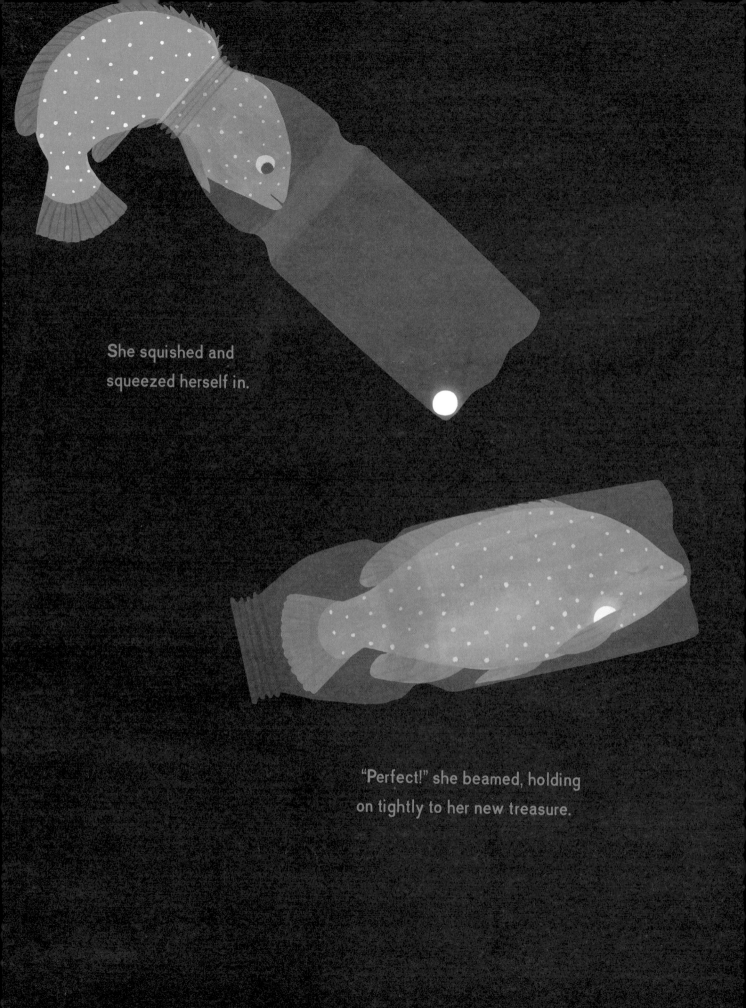

She squished and
squeezed herself in.

"Perfect!" she beamed, holding
on tightly to her new treasure.

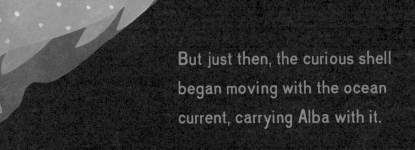

But just then, the curious shell began moving with the ocean current, carrying Alba with it.

No amount of wriggling would set her free, and all she could do was drift.

Finally, Alba floated to the surface, where a peculiar
new world appeared. Giant creatures moved on the
surface of the water and white lights shone through
the darkness.

Alba saw hundreds of smaller objects too.
They looked just like the ones that had littered the reef.

She looked across at the lights, and
longed to go home. That night she
dreamt of her old spotted shell nestled
within the city of coral.

The next morning, a little girl was walking along the beach looking for beautiful objects for her collection. But it wasn't a shiny treasure she found, it was Alba.

She looked at the barely moving fish trapped in the bottle. "I'll get you out," she said. Then she looked at the plastic bottles and bags scattered over the beach. "This must have come from my town."

She realised she had to do something. "I think it's time to tidy up."

Alba wriggled in her hands. "Don't worry. I'll put you back in the ocean as soon as it's safe."

The girl rescued Alba from the bottle and put her in clean water. When people asked about the orange fish, the girl told them how Alba was found. Soon everyone realised they had to change the way they lived.

The whole town worked together to clear up
the mess. They cleaned and cleaned and bit
by bit, piece by piece, the sea started to get
a little brighter again.

Once the ocean was clean enough for Alba to return, the girl said goodbye and released her back into the water.

Alba was excited to go home. "What will it be like now?" she wondered. And, still clutching her precious pearl, she went in search of her old spotted shell and her collection of treasures.

When she reached her old home, she found that most of
the strange objects had gone. It was clean!
On Alba's one hundredth birthday, she celebrated with
her friends among a world of coral that was becoming
busy and bright again.

Alba's new addition to her collection dazzled
her guests. As they gathered round the pearl,
she told them a story all about a brave little girl
who loved to play by a brilliant blue ocean.

Did you spot . . . ?

The coral reef is home to some of the most colourful and unique wildlife in the world.
Go back through the book and see if you can spot some of Alba's ocean friends.

SPOTTED MORAY EEL

(Gymnothorax moringa)

Rocky surfaces with hidden crevices are
the ideal locations for this snake-like
creature to hide in. A solitary hunter, the
spotted moray eel has poor eyesight but an
excellent sense of smell and a toxic bite.

BLUECHEEK BUTTERFLYFISH

(Chaetodon semilarvatus)

A common sight on the coral reef, this
striking fish mates with one partner for
life, and as such can often be found
swimming in a pair. Its tiny snout is
perfect for nibbling at coral polyps
and eating small worms.

RED SPOTTED CORAL CRAB

(Trapezia tigrina)

Don't be fooled by those brightly
coloured polka dots. These feisty
crustaceans fiercely guard their
coral reef homes.

EMPEROR ANGELFISH

(Pomacanthus imperator)

This flat-bodied fish feeds on algae and
sponges. As it grows into an adult, the
patterns on its body become a light, yellowish
green, edged with vibrant electric blue.

GREATER BLUE-RINGED OCTOPUS

(Hapalochlaena lunulata)

The stunning patterns on this tiny octopus
warn predators to stay away – it is highly
venomous. It lives in burrows on the
ocean floor, which it only leaves at
night to search for food.

PINK DORID NUDIBRANCH

(Chromodoris bullocki)

Nudibranches are among some of the most stunning species of sea slug in the world. Their vivid colours and textures have developed to blend in with their coral reef surroundings.

VIOLET SPOTTED REEF LOBSTER

(Enoplometopus debelius)

This beautifully patterned reef lobster only grows to about 15cm. It lives in warm, tropical oceans near rocky surfaces and comes out to hunt at night.

LEAFY SEA DRAGON

(Phycodurus eques)

This clever seahorse looks just like seaweed and is perfectly suited to the kelp forests in which it lives. The male leafy sea dragon looks after the babies, known as fry.

BLUE SEASTAR

(Linckia laevigata)

With arms covered in suckers, this starfish creeps along the ocean floor, attaching itself to rocks and coral in the hope of catching a passing meal.

OCELLARIS CLOWNFISH

(Amphiprion ocellaris)

These little fish can only be found on coral reefs. They live amongst the tentacles of sea anemones and have a mucus layer that protects them from the anemones' stings.

Looking after our oceans

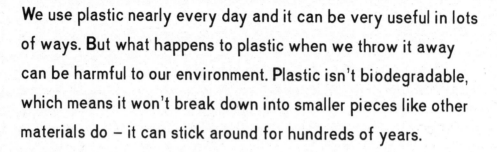

We use plastic nearly every day and it can be very useful in lots of ways. But what happens to plastic when we throw it away can be harmful to our environment. Plastic isn't biodegradable, which means it won't break down into smaller pieces like other materials do – it can stick around for hundreds of years.

When plastic washes up in the ocean, it can harm the animals that live there. Plastic bags can be mistaken for jellyfish and so they are eaten by whales and turtles, while smaller creatures can choke on plastic straws and ring-pull cans can cut or damage fish. There are lots of ways in which we can look after our oceans. Here are a few things you can do to help:

1. Use fewer plastic products

2. Help take care of beaches

3. Influence change in the community

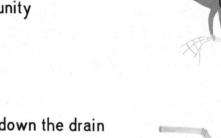

4. Re-use and recycle

5. Never pour harmful chemicals down the drain